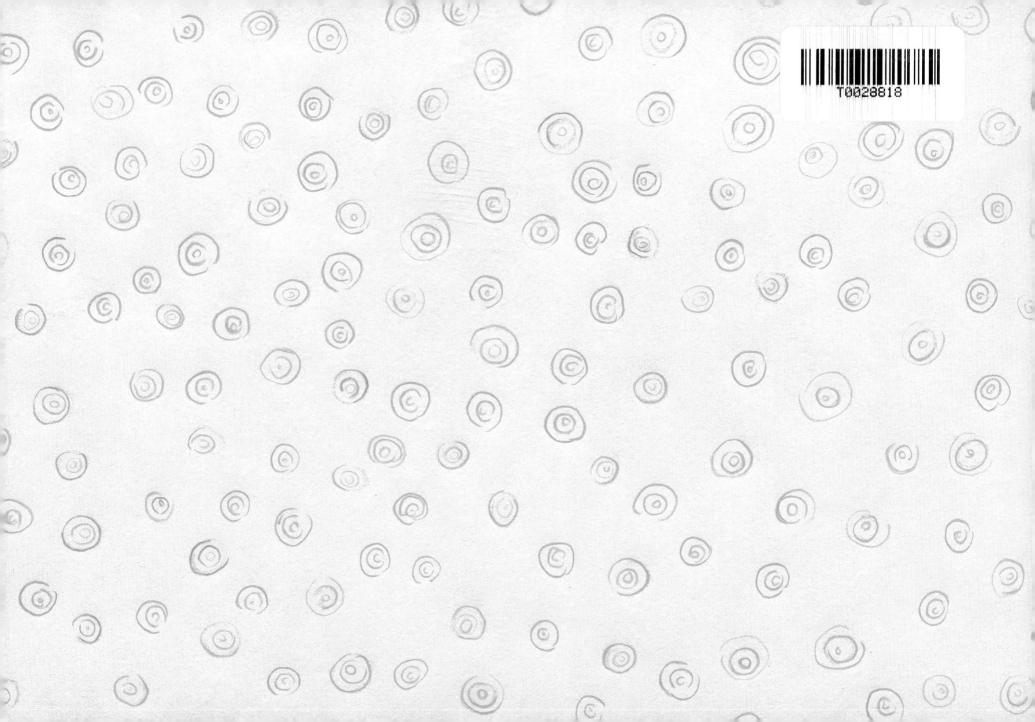

Text and illustrations copyright © 2021 by Eva Montanari

Tundra Books, an imprint of Penguin Random House Canada Young Readers, a division of Penguin Random House of Canada Limited

Originally published in the UK as *What Does the Crocodile Say?* in 2018 by Book Island.

Library and Archives Canada Cataloguing in Publication

Title: What does the little crocodile say? / written and illustrated by Eva Montanari.
Names: Montanari, Eva, 1977- author, illustrator.
Identifiers: Canadiana (print) 20200231545 | Canadiana (ebook) 20200231553 | ISBN 9780735268135
  (hardcover) | ISBN 9780735268142 (EPUB)
Classification: LCC PZ7.M763 Whc 2021 | DDC j823/.92—dc23

Published simultaneously in the United States of America by Tundra Books of Northern New York, an imprint of Penguin Random House Canada Young Readers, a division of Penguin Random House of Canada Limited

Library of Congress Control Number: 2020936952

North American edition edited by Samantha Swenson
North American edition designed by Kate Sinclair
The artwork in this book was rendered in colored pencil and chalk pastels.
Hand lettering by Eva Montanari

Printed and bound in China

www.penguinrandomhouse.ca

1 2 3 4 5   25 24 23 22 21

Penguin
Random House
tundra | TUNDRA BOOKS

To Debbie for loving this story
and to Ruggero who inspired it!

WHAT DOES LITTLE CROCODILE SAY?

Eva Montanari

tundra

THE ALARM CLOCK
GOES RING RING.

THE TICKLE GOES TEE-HEE.

THE WATER GOES SPLASH.

THE ZIPPER
GOES ZZZT.

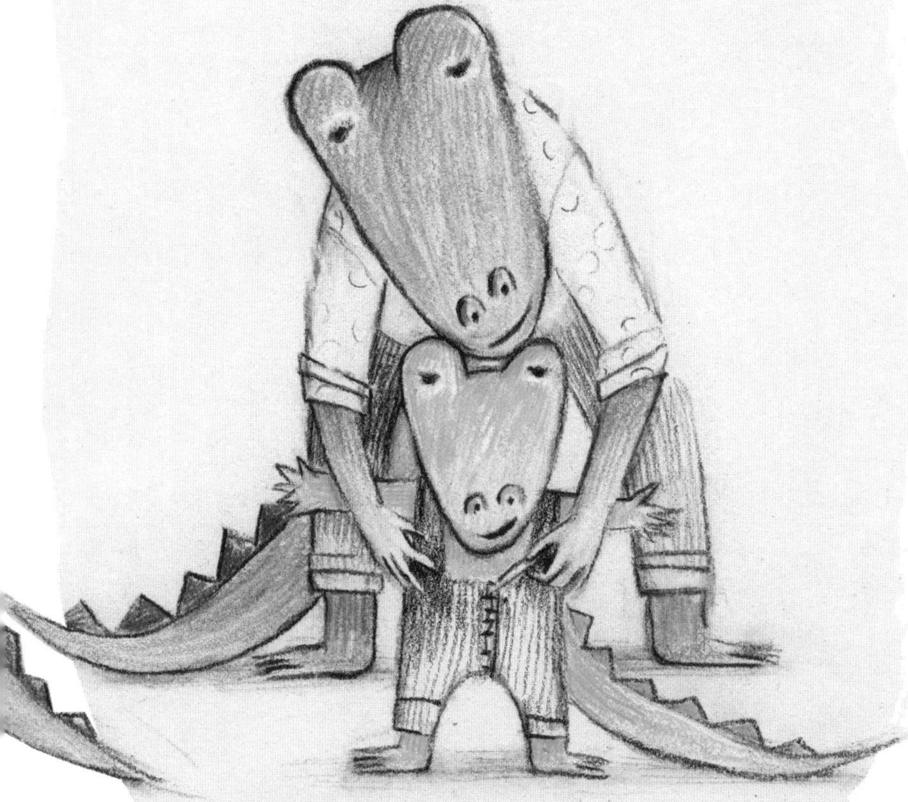

THE COOKIE
GOES PLOP.

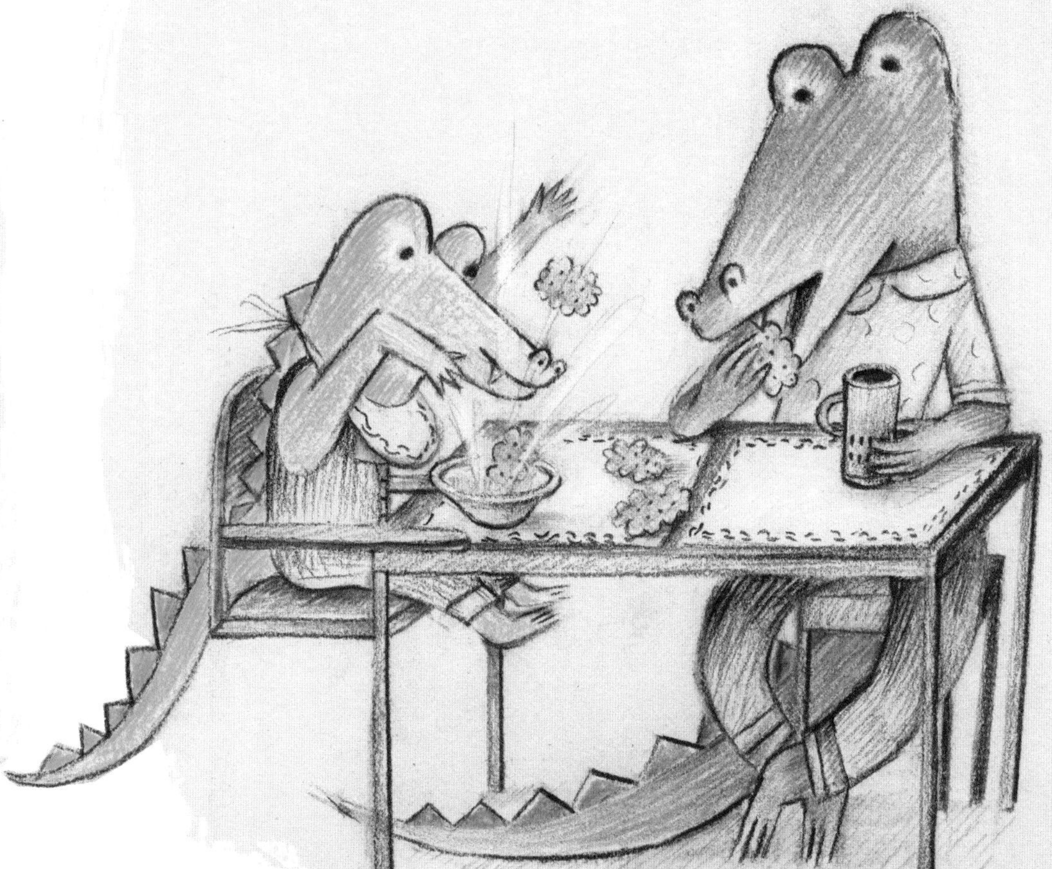

THE DOOR GOES WUMP.

THE CAR GOES VROOM VROOM.

THE CAR DOOR
GOES BLEEP.

THE BELL GOES
DING-DONG.

THE ELEPHANT SAYS GOOD MORNING!

THE STAIRS GO HUP HUP.

THE PIG SAYS OINK OINK.
THE CAT SAYS MEOW.
THE BIRD SAYS TWEET TWEET.
THE FROG SAYS RIBBIT.
THE WOLF SAYS
AROOOO!

AND WHAT DOES
LITTLE CROCODILE SAY?

THE BOOK GOES
ONCE UPON A TIME...

THE DRUM GOES
RAT-A-TAT RAT-A-TAT
RAT-A-TAT RAT-A-TAT.

THE TRUMPET
GOES PAH-PA-RAH.

THE TRIANGLE GOES TING.

THE FOOD GOES
NOM NOM NOM.

THE MILK GOES
GLUG GLUG GLUG.

THE NAP GOES Zzz Zzz

THE BUBBLES GO....

THE DOOR GOES
KNOCK KNOCK.

BIG CROCODILE SAYS PEEKABOO!

AND WHAT
DOES LITTLE
CROCODILE SAY?

THE FAREWELL GOES

SEE YOU TOMORROW!